The Youngest Fairy Godmother Ever

BY
Stephen Krensky

ILLUSTRATED BY
Diana Cain Bluthenthal

Simon & Schuster Books for Young Readers

Artist's Note
The artwork was created using
a mixture of inks and paints.

 SIMON & SCHUSTER BOOKS FOR YOUNG READERS
An imprint of Simon & Schuster Children's Publishing Division
1230 Avenue of the Americas, New York, New York 10020
Text copyright © 2000 by Stephen Krensky
Illustrations copyright © 2000 by Diana Cain Bluthenthal
Book design by Paul Zakris. The text of this book is set in 18-point Filosofia.
Printed in Hong Kong
10 9 8 7 6 5 4 3 2 1

Library of Congress Cataloging-in-Publication Data

Krensky, Stephen.
The youngest fairy godmother ever / by Stephen Krensky ;
illustrated by Diana Cain Bluthenthal. — 1st ed.
p.   cm.
Summary: Mavis tries to pursue her goal of playing fairy godmother and granting
wishes to those around her, but she finds the process trickier than she thought.
ISBN 0-689-82011-9 (hardcover)
[1. Wishes—Fiction. 2. Fairies—Fiction.] I. Bluthenthal, Diana Cain, ill. II. Title.
PZ7.K883Yo 2000
[E]—dc21
98-22750
CIP
AC

 first edition

For my mother, who also likes
to make wishes come true.
-S.K.

Dedicated with love to Vince, Cameron, and Kelley—
three dream-boat wishes come true! Special thanks
to my own fairy godmother, who delivers prayers
from my lips to God's ears.
-D.C.B.

On Career Day at school,
Mavis Trumble heard all about shooting rockets into space,
hunting for dinosaur bones,
and designing the latest computer games.

Some kids had trouble deciding which job they liked best.
The new girl, Cindy, said she felt like she had too many
jobs already.

But not Mavis. Her plans were set.
When she grew up she wanted to be a fairy godmother.
"Because," she said, "I want to make wishes come true."

Her parents were delighted.

"You can start by taking out the trash," said Mr. Trumble.

"And cleaning your room," Mrs. Trumble added.

Mavis just shook her head.

She was sure wishes like that didn't count.

Laura from next door wondered how hard the job would be.

"You might have to work day and night," she said.

"It'll be worth it," Mavis insisted.

In fact, Mavis started practicing the very next day.
Since fairy godmothers watched over people in secret,
she learned to blend into the background.

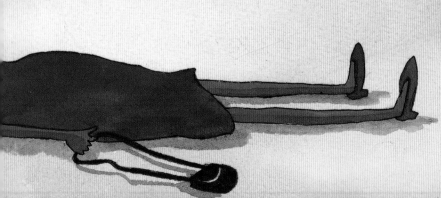

She also spent time popping up out of nowhere.

But the hardest thing to figure out
was the right way to grant wishes.
This is very tricky, thought Mavis.
What if I grant someone the wrong wish by mistake?

Or what if a person wanted one thing
but later changed his mind?

But she had to start somewhere.

"Can you help me become a circus star?" Laura asked.

"I want people to 'Ooooh!' and 'Ahhhh!' over my every move."

Mavis decided to try.

She rounded up their friends for the show.

"Ooooh!" they shouted when Mavis signaled them.

The sudden noise surprised Laura.

OOOOOOOOOOH!!

OOOOH!!

AAAAAAAAHHHH!!

Luckily, the umbrella broke her fall.
"*Ahhhh!*" said the kids together.
Mavis sighed. She could see Laura was not pleased.

After that Mavis decided she needed to learn more,
so she went to the library.

She found out about special costumes and magic wands
and wishing really hard with her eyes squeezed shut.

Mavis got her costume and wand ready.
She waved the wand around to test its weight and balance.

And since fairy godmothers were wise and kind,
Mavis practiced making the right expressions.

Finally, it was time to try her magic.

At school Mavis took Hector out of his cage.
She closed her eyes and imagined Hector turning into a
coachman—just like the mice in the stories she had read.

When she opened her eyes, she didn't see a coachman.
She didn't see Hector, either.

It took the whole class to find him.

Mavis had to stay after school to clean up the mess.
Cindy offered to help her.
"I do a lot of cleaning up at home," she explained.

Mavis was very grateful.

The next day their teacher announced
the school's annual Halloween party.
Everyone was excited—everyone except Cindy.
"What's the matter?" Mavis asked. "Don't you like parties?"
"Oh, yes," said Cindy. "And I'm sure my stepsisters will go.
They always have the most beautiful costumes.
But I don't have anything to wear."

Mavis smiled. Here was a wish she could handle.

Of course, Mavis still had a long way to go.
This magic stuff was bound to be tricky.

She might not be a fairy godmother yet . . .

. . . but she was off to a very good start.